A Note to Parents and Caregivers:

Read-it! Readers are for children who are just starting on the amazing road to reading. These beautiful books support both the acquisition of reading skills and the love of books.

 The PURPLE LEVEL presents basic topics and objects using high frequency words and simple language patterns.

 The RED LEVEL presents familiar topics using common words and repeating sentence patterns.

 The BLUE LEVEL presents new ideas using a larger vocabulary and varied sentence structure.

 The YELLOW LEVEL presents more challenging ideas, a broad vocabulary, and wide variety in sentence structure.

 The GREEN LEVEL presents more complex ideas, an extended vocabulary range, and expanded language structures.

 The ORANGE LEVEL presents a wide range of ideas and concepts using challenging vocabulary and complex language structures.

When sharing a book with your child, read in short stretches, pausing often to talk about the pictures. Have your child turn the pages and point to the pictures and familiar words. And be sure to reread favorite stories or parts of stories.

There is no right or wrong way to share books with children. Find time to read with your child, and pass on the legacy of literacy.

Adria F. Klein, Ph.D.
Professor Emeritus
California State University
San Bernardino, California

Editor: Christianne C. Jones
Designer: Amy Bailey Muehlenhardt
Page Production: Tracy Kaehler
Creative Director: Keith Griffin
Editorial Director: Carol Jones
The illustrations in this book were created with watercolor and pencil.

Picture Window Books
5115 Excelsior Boulevard
Suite 232
Minneapolis, MN 55416
877-845-8392
www.picturewindowbooks.com

Printed in the United States of America.

Library of Congress Cataloging-in-Publication Data
Blackaby, Susan.
Coco on the go / by Susan Blackaby ; illustrated by Amy Bailey Muehlenhardt.
p. cm. — (Read-it! readers)
Summary: Coco the dog goes everywhere with Mama and the new baby, but at the
end of the day, Coco and the baby want different things.
ISBN 1-4048-1580-5 (hardcover)
[1. Babies—Fiction. 2. Dogs—Fiction.] I. Muehlenhardt, Amy Bailey, 1974-, ill.
II. Title. III. Series.

PZ7.B5318Coc 2005
[E]—dc22   2005021443

CoCo on the Go

by Susan Blackaby
illustrated by Amy Bailey Muehlenhardt

Special thanks to our advisers for their expertise:

Adria F. Klein, Ph.D.
Professor Emeritus, California State University
San Bernardino, California

Susan Kesselring, M.A.
Literacy Educator
Rosemount–Apple Valley–Eagan (Minnesota) School District

PICTURE WINDOW BOOKS
Minneapolis, Minnesota

Coco goes where Mom goes.

Elise goes, too.

5

Coco walks in the neighborhood.

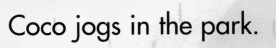

Coco jogs in the park.

Coco splashes and swims
in the water.

11

Coco rides in a basket
on the front of the bike.

Coco plays in the car.

Coco stops and begs for fish.

17

At the end of the day,
Coco feels sleepy.

19

Coco wants to rest.

But Elise wants to play.

More *Read-it!* Readers

Bright pictures and fun stories help you practice your reading skills. Look for more books at your level.

Ann Plants a Garden 1-4048-1010-2
The Babysitter 1-4048-1187-7
Bess and Tess 1-4048-1013-7
The Best Soccer Player 1-4048-1055-2
Dan Gets Set 1-4048-1011-0
Fishing Trip 1-4048-1004-8
Jen Plays 1-4048-1008-0
Joey's First Day 1-4048-1174-5
Just Try It 1-4048-1175-3
Mary's Art 1-4048-1056-0
The Missing Tooth 1-4048-1592-9
Moving Day 1-4048-1006-4
Pat Picks Up 1-4048-1059-5
A Place for Mike 1-4048-1012-9
Room to Share 1-4048-1185-0
Shopping for Lunch 1-4048-1589-9
Syd's Room 1-4048-1585-6
Wes Gets a Pet 1-4048-1060-9
Winter Fun for Kat 1-4048-1007-2
A Year of Fun 1-4048-1009-9

Looking for a specific title or level? A complete list of *Read-it!* Readers is available on our Web site:
www.picturewindowbooks.com